TIME WASTERS #1

TIME WASTERS BOOK 1

DIDI OVIATT

Copyright (C) 2017 Didi Oviatt

Layout design and Copyright (C) 2021 by Next Chapter

Published 2021 by Next Chapter

Edited by Tyler Colins

Cover art by CoverMint

Back cover texture by David M. Schrader, used under license from Shutterstock.com

This book is a work of fiction. Names, characters, places, and incidents are the product of the author's imagination or are used fictitiously. Any resemblance to actual events, locales, or persons, living or dead, is purely coincidental.

All rights reserved. No part of this book may be reproduced or transmitted in any form or by any means, electronic or mechanical, including photocopying, recording, or by any information storage and retrieval system, without the author's permission.

TIME WASTERS
BOOK ONE

Super Short Preludes
Love or Low Places
Sabotage by Hook & Dog
Trampling Beast
Didi Oviatt

ABOUT THE AUTHOR AND THE SERIES

Didi Oviatt is a small-town gal who married a small-town guy. Within a few years of experiencing a new family's bliss, she discovered that she had a thirst to write. Now, after digging down deep and getting in touch with her literary self, she's writing thrillers like **Search For Maylee**, **Justice for Belle**, **Aggravated Momentum**, **Sketch**, and **New Age Lamians**.

The *Time Wasters Series* are all titled *Super Short Prelude* because they ARE just that - super short stories that lead up to big life concepts or events. Designed to help pass short spurts of time, most of the *Time Wasters* stories range from 8 to 15 pages. Each contains an entire story that will draw you in, make you laugh, and then allow you to move on with your life. If you want to read, but don't have the time, or are in no mood for a "Novel Commitment", then a Time Waster is just what you need.

STORY ONE

LOVE OR LOW PLACES? SUPER SHORT PRELUDE TO LOVE

Based on a true story, this super short tale of love offers a harsh, humorous, and yet somehow touching glimpse into what could possibly be the norm for young couples today. The Time Wasters Series brings about several Super Short Prelude Stories (names have been altered to protect identities) In Love or Low Places: Dana is young, wild, careless and free, that is until her entire world is turned upside down by a man she meets at karaoke night. Is there really such thing as love at first sight? You be the judge.

The liquid in my glass peeks up me with its rank whiskey scent and its tempting golden bronze shimmer. The time is creeping up on midnight and I'm slightly drunker than usual for this hour. Despite my argument to stay in, my roommate Lynn lays on the pressure pretty thick.

"Dana," she snaps a finger between my fixated eyes and the spot on the wall they're staring at. "Pay attention."

"Ugh."

I may be growling, but trust me, it's in a fun, loving way. I accept the shot of Jägermeister that she eagerly slides across the counter at me. It's swallowed in one gulp and chased by the last lingering drop of watered-down Jack and Pepsi in my other hand. I shudder, gag, hold my breath to stop the forming puke at the base of my neck, and then giggle a little. *That was a close one.*

"Wow, Lynn, you're like a gnat," I tease.

"Well, my God. My kids are with their dad, and I don't have to work tonight. We don't even have to go to *our* bar; we can drive to different one."

I mull her proposition over carefully. There aren't many other bars around. We'd have to make the thirty-minute drive to the county over and, even there, the options are limited. It's a Wednesday night, meaning there'll be karaoke at the tiny little hotel bar inside the Holiday Inn. There's usually a decent crowd at karaoke night. No matter how stiff my intentions start out to remain at home, I always manage to have a good time when we go out. The bulky, beaded purple and silver watch on my wrist reads 11:50 P.M. and last call is always at 2:00 A.M. This means if I kill another thirty minutes, then we'll only have an hour to drink at the bar once we get there. It also means Lynn will be slightly irritated and on the pissy side for the majority of the ride over, so it'll give me something to poke fun at.

"I don't know, Lynn. Just not sure I'm feeling it."

I'm lying, I know full well I'll go.

"So, what should we do?" she pushes. "Have a couple more shots, stare at each other, and then pass out before one? I'm bored as shit, don't be an asshole."

I can't help but to laugh at her. She smirks an unintentional grin and then lowers her brows on purpose, making an awkward effort to glower.

"You can go if you want. Don't let me hold you back," I insist.

"Are you shitting me right now?"

"Nope," I say as I make my way to the fridge to grab another beer. "I've had enough as it is. I don't think I can handle much more alcohol tonight. I'll just stay home and finish off this last beer before bed."

It's working, only a few more minutes of making her wait and I'll go. Soon, she'll be good and irritated, and I'll be drunk enough not to spend any money at the bar. The stool I plop myself back down on sits directly across from her, so I have a very close view of her body growing in need of a tantrum: flexed arms are folded across her chest and there is a slight vibration in her hips. It doesn't matter that her legs are hidden by the wrap-around kitchen bar between us; it's clear that she's tapping her foot like a five-year-old. I chuckle while she shakes her head and pours another shot. This time she keeps it to herself, no sharing *her* bottle, and no more pushy words (yet). I slowly take another very small sip of my beer. *Wait for it ... wait for it ...*

Then she snaps under pressure.

"Damn it, Dana. Please!" She unsuccessfully tries to keep control of her raising voice. "Please don't make me go by myself. You can't even tell me *no* without laughing. You're just wasting time to be a dick!"

The jig is up, I guess she has me all figured out. I take another slow sip before my reluctant agreement to go. "Okay, okay. Just let me finish this one beer first."

The ride is as expected. The first half is full of loud music and stiff torsos, both of us staring blankly ahead. The second half we're finally able to joke about our late start on the night and share a few completely inappropriate memories and jokes to lighten the mood. By the time the slow-moving wheels of Lynn's car very cautiously find a space in the hotel parking lot, we are both laughing to the near point of peeing our pants. Then it hits. My stomach completely flips before I can even step out of the car. A whoosh of drunken nausea works its way from my head to my toes and leaves the seat to swirl beneath me.

"Shit Lynn, I think I'm gonna puke." I reach for the car handle and lean out.

"What the hell? We haven't even went inside yet."

She hides her growing smile with a closed fist and chuckles under her breath at my stupidity. Ever so patiently, she sits in the driver's seat, just waiting for her partner in crime to pull herself together.

With one foot on the spinning pavement and one still in the car, I lean into the fresh air and wrap an arm around my stomach. Nothing. No throw up yet. *I think I might be okay.* The sound of her pitchy chuckle rings through the car. It bounces off the windshield and slams me in the face.

"What the hell is so funny?" I manage to ask. "I started hours before you did."

"You should see your face." She no longer hides the chuckle; instead she lets an overbearing laugh escape her. "I think your lips are actually white."

As luck may have it, I'm able to hold down the growing acidic fluid at the base of my throat long enough to go inside. I make my way straight to the bathroom and rid myself of the previous two hours worth of liquid that had entered my body. Music echoes in my ears as the last round of vomit fills the toilet. A very distinct tune of "I've Got Friends In Low Places" by Garth Brooks pushes through the air in waves. *Well, if this isn't ironic, then I don't know what is.* The sparkles on the back pocket of my jeans press against the tiles, and my head falls back to grace the metal public bathroom stall. *Classy.*

I blow my nose and wipe the involuntary puke tears from my soaked cheeks and listen. I imagine the words to this appropriately fitting song to be sung by Garth himself rather than the off-key group of clearly drunken men that are slurring and shouting into microphones. I'm quite sure they're even hanging on each other and making it an unspoken competition to see who can make their voice the lowest and twangiest. *Men, can't live with 'em, can't feed 'em whiskey,* I think.

Whew, at least I'm starting to feel better. I'm actually glad I threw up, because I just so happen to be one of those weirdos that are like a whole new woman after a good puke. I bounce back like a fresh new rubber band, ready to conquer the night. My second wind is a force to be reckoned with. I'm sure when I'm old, I'll look back and realize how naive and self-destructive my invincible drinking habits were. But, for now I'll enjoy my bounce-back abilities as the young vibrant free-spirited soul that I am.

After pulling myself to a standing position, I shake it off, literally. I wiggle my body a bit just to make sure the motion won't cause another round. It doesn't, I'm golden. The motion nausea is gone, as is the spinning of ground under my feet. I jump up and down, but only twice, and only a couple of inches; my coordination doesn't allow much more than that when I'm sober, let alone now.

I feel nearly one hundred percent again. Still drunk, but

not sick. I wash my hands and face, touch up my make-up and then throw in a fresh stick of gum. No one will ever know of my barfing extravaganza, aside from Lynn. Unless of course she announces it into one of those irritating microphones, with my odds at this point being 50/50.

A creaky door swings easily to let me into the main room of the bar. The wide open space is split down the middle. To my right, one whole side of the bar is full of round wooden tables encased with chairs that are covered in a thick, itchy colorful canvas that may be better placed on the floor of a casino. To my left is the actual bar, and two pool tables with an abundance of men, no women, standing around it, holding cue sticks. On the far end of the room is a stage. I try not to look too closely, as the chords of Garth's song is *still* being twanged and roughly giggled through; *my hell, it's a long song.*

I spot Lynn sitting ever so casually at a mid-sized round table close to the bar. She's sipping on the cheapest beer available; there is another one on the table waiting for me, and her eyes are practically glued to her phone. I assume she's texting everyone she knows, trying to convince them to join us for the last hour of drinks before last call. It's an easy play to call. I close the gap between us and take my seat.

"Any luck?" I ask.

"Nope, everyone is being little bitches."

"Well, it is after midnight ... on a Wednesday," I tease and take a big gulp of my beer, letting it wash down the tasteless gum in my mouth.

"Hag," she mumbles. "I hope we can find a good afterparty."

"Yeah, me too, actually. I feel much better now."

"I'm sure you do." She giggles.

Finally, the longest Garth Brooks song in the history of country music comes to an end and I look up to see him. That's right, *HIM*. The twangiest voice of the bunch was sung by none other than the man of my dreams. All beard and no embarrassment. They're slapping one another's backs after their proud display of *"Low Places"*.

"Look at him," I tell her.

"Which one?" Her head snaps up like a lioness on the prowl.

"Far left, Yankee's hat."

She tilts her head in thought, "Yeah, he's alright I guess."

"Alright?" I can't believe her. "Just alright? He's a ten!"

"Dana, I don't think anyone in this bar tonight is a ten." Then she returns her attention to her phone and spits out some statement that I only hear half of. "Just don't leave me at this ..."

I'm out of my seat before she has the chance to finish. She may have said "table" and ended it there, or maybe she said "table without getting me a drink". Who knows? I'm distracted and far too busy honing in on my prize. His small group splits; some make their way to the pool tables, some to bar stools. I linger in close behind until he takes a seat, then I cram myself between him and some other burly looking guy who took the stool next to his. There's no stool for me to sit on, so I'm forced to stand shoulder to shoulder between them. I bury myself in the scent of his cologne and then allow my entire left side to feel the heat of his body.

Without any words, I tell him hello with only a smile and undress-me eyes. A fraction of me is shy, which is weird and completely out of the ordinary. Another part of me is overwhelmed by excitement and the embarrassing question as to whether he'll be able to tell that I just barfed my guts out. I lean over the bar to draw the attention of the woman behind it and, of course, to give this enticing man a good look at my rear end. I order us each one shot and one beer. The rest of the night is history. We're inseparable. We laugh, we drink, we dance, we drink, we make plans to go fishing the very next day, and we drink some more.

Then, comes the kiss. That's right, we're kissing after I puked. In all fairness, it's been a few hours and a lot of after-party alcohol since my public bathroom episode.

He is an amazing kisser! I don't even mind the beard. I can't recall ever feeling this way after just one kiss. I want to crawl inside his arms and live there. If not forever, then at least for a season. I want to hibernate against his engulfing heat. I want to drink in the scent of him and relive this kiss every second for the rest of my life. There is no doubt in my mind that this man is to be mine forever, and that's final.

STORY TWO

SABOTAGE BY HOOK & DOG, SUPER SHORT PRELUDE TO ADVENTURE

Based on a true story, this super short tale of adventure offers the humorous insight of a couple's competitive banter, along with the shocking details of a fish-hook disaster. The Time Wasters Series brings about several Super Short Prelude Stories (names have been altered to protect identities). In Sabotage by Hook and Dog, Dani convinces her husband, brother-in-law and friend to go on a fishing adventure, only to have a disastrous turn of events completely take over.

There's a certain moisture in the air of my house, and it's a little irritating. It makes the doors tight in their frames, and the fruit in the wicker basket on my kitchen counter ripen way too fast. I grocery shop one day, and then I'll have brown bananas and moldy bread by the very next evening. Sometimes, on days that it's really hot outside, there'll even be a damp, sticky soap film on the floor. It's caused by the re-wetted Pine-Sol from mopping in the morning while it's still dry; then, the humidity shows up and by early afternoon it's taken over, consuming the once cleanliness of my house. I hate swamp coolers.

Every summer, it's the same thing. I swear if I ever move again, it'll be to a house with a gigantic yard and no swamp cooler. My friends and family claim they don't notice how muggy the air is, but honestly, I think they're just being dirty little liars. I mean, really, how could you *not* notice? Oh well, I guess no harm no foul. I suppose I won't hold their attempt at kindness against them.

Today is one of those extra hot days. I can even taste the dankness of the air's moisture as it rolls into my mouth with each breath. My three-year-old runs past me, through the living room. I can hear the *thomp, thomp, thomp* of his feet hitting the hardwood. *I can't do this, not today.* I can't allow myself to sit around the house and pass my time by listening to the loud water pushing cooler, forced cold air into the few rooms in its range.

I stomp to the large window of my living room that takes up the majority of the wall, and I yank open the tall maroon colored curtains. Light pours in, causing my husband, Carlos, to squint his eyes tightly, and a crease to form in the bunched-up skin between his brows.

"Why? Wife? Just, why?" he sarcastically moans.

"Get up and put your shoes on," I demand with my toes tapping impatiently on the sticky floor. An amused smirk grows across my face. "We have to go out and do something today, or I'm gonna lose my shit."

"Well, nobody wants that," he teases. "Did you really have to open the curtains without warning like that? I think I'm blind."

Just as I'm about to retort with some smart remark about how it was utterly necessary to make him uncomfortable in order to get the ball rolling, he's saved by the sound of tires pulling into our driveway. I turn and look through the very window that I'd just used to disrupt my husband's comfort. The tall window just so happens to be all that separates us from the driveway, so it offers a clear view.

"Yes!" I proclaim. "Todd and Maria are here. I was starting to wonder if they'd ever show up. Maybe they'll wanna go fishing or something."

Carlos leans forward and kicks the extended footrest of his recliner back to its rightful upright position.

"What about the kids?" he asks with a pinched face. "You really wanna take 'em fishing *again* this week?" There's a real emphasis on again.

"Maybe," I respond with utter honesty. "Probably not though; it's kind of a pain in the ass. Plus, your mom said she'd take 'em today if we want her to."

Our kids are three and eleven months old, and taking them on extended adventures really is kind of hard, especially fishing. The amount of necessities to be carried from the vehicle to the water, no matter how far it may be, seems to quadruple when they're involved. There are diaper bags, snacks, bottles, milk and juice cooler, chairs, and blankets.

Every item needs to be at arm's length at all times, and that's not to mention the crying, whining, and poop-changing on hard rocky grounds and, of course, the tangling or snagging of fishing lines. Granted, seeing those thrilled little faces when they get to reel in a fish is arguably the cutest and most exciting thing on the face of the earth. Although it usually makes all the hassle worthwhile, I think the mood of today is leaning more towards freedom. A good well-rounded break from the kiddos is a luxury that's not to be taken lightly.

Carlos and I knew his brother, Todd, would be coming over at some point, but weren't really sure exactly when. Don't even ask about the obvious conflict of their names; that's a mess all in its own.

Now, strutting to our front door in front of Todd, is my close friend Maria. Her legs are long and bare, aside from the Levi jean shorts and the tall black and turquoise cowboy boots that stretch nearly to her knees. Todd drags his feet slowly behind her; there's obviously no hurry in his step. In his arms is her beautiful yet fairly mean, pure white Jack Russell dog, Sophie. In no time at all, Maria comes bounding through the door.

"Hey Dani." She beams.

"Yo," I respond, before dramatically plopping myself on the couch.

She glances back and forth between the two of us, the wheels clearly turning in her head. It doesn't take long for her to pick up on the restless look in my gaze, nor the playfully irritated up-turn of Carlos' lip. No sooner does Todd come traipsing in behind her, when Maria waves her arms in an exaggerated circle around herself and says with a gigantic grin, "Who's ready to embrace the day!?"

Todd steps past her, rolls his eyes, chuckles, and then gives her a wink. After a somewhat heated exploration of options, the four of us put our heads together and make a plan. Ultimately, I win out, as usual, and we decide to fish at a lake, not a river, and without the kids. The area we live in is beautiful and our options truly are amazing. We're very blessed to be able to enjoy an outdoorsy lifestyle. The air of our nearby mountains is pure, and an incomparable red-sanded desert is just as close, and equally as majestic.

The six of us squeeze into Carlos' trusty F-150 amongst diaper bags and fishing gear, with Sophie in tow. For being a mid-sized truck, it's surprisingly spacious. Carlos drives with Maria and Todd at his side in the front seat, and I squeeze into the backseat with all of our stuff between the two kids in their luxury car seats.

Normally, I'd offer to hold Sophie in the back seat with me and the kids, as not to distract the driver, but I don't because she hates me. Sophie practically hates anyone who isn't Maria. I really struggle with this dog. But Maria loves her like a human baby, and she's loyal, so I guess I'll give her a pass. Sophie is jumpy with strangers and a nipper. She also isn't too particularly fond of kids, so having my not-so-cautious toddlers pawing at her in a tightly enclosed area may not be the best idea.

No sooner are my children safely in the arms and home of their grandmother, when I resume my rightful place in the front seat and crack open a beer. I'm determined to have a fantastic day in the sun, by enjoying a few ice cold ones and, hopefully, catching the holy-mother-loving-monster of all fish. If nothing else, I had better at least catch something bigger than Carlos, because that sucker out-fishes me every single time. I'm really looking forward to not having to chase around the kids today. Now, I can actually cast out my pole out more than once.

It's about a forty-five-minute drive from the in-laws' house to the lake. We blare the type of music mix that honestly should be admired by any and everyone. Everything from sixties country, to eighties rock, to nineties rap, to current pop is shuffled through and blasted out of the speakers. Whether it be awkward or well-rounded, either way it works. Maria belts every word from the back seat, twanging or pitching her voice as necessary. I never can decide whether I'm more impressed or jealous by Maria's ability to retain. This girl could hear a song one time and then turn around and sing every word a week later.

The second small town between home and the lake is passed, and we round a corner that leads to the mouth of a winding canyon. Tall pointy mountains range on either side of the road; we're separated from them by a few hay fields. The edging where hay fields meet mountain bases are full of cedar trees, vibrant tall grass, and a few spread-out patches of violet wildflowers. Off the drivers' side, there is also a small flowing river. I look to my left and spot a mama mule deer and her fawn a couple dozen yards from the road. It's beautiful. I absolutely love where I live.

"You know, I'm gonna catch the biggest fish today, right?" I turn and smugly announce to Carlos, hardly able to hold back a smile.

"My ass," he retorts with a stone face, not missing a beat.

Maria instantly pauses her singing to join in the healthy competition. "Loser buys dinner—you suckers are going down!"

"If that's the case," Carlos says with a slight competitive giggle, "Then I'm not helping either of you gals bait your poles or untangle your lines."

"Me either," Todd pipes up.

"Deal," I agree.

"Who needs a man anyway, right, Dani?!" Maria shouts playfully.

"Yes!" I completely agree.

Rather than continuing with what's started out to be a potential battle of the sexes (that the women would obviously win), Carlos laughs at our tenacity and cranks the radio back up. Maria jumps right back into her word-for-word role play of the blaring alternative song. I crack open another beer and resume my admiration of the mountains. The farther we climb up the elevation scale, the prettier the scenery becomes.

The roadside pebbles have transformed into boulders, and the small flowing stream has changed into a beautiful cascade of winding, white water. It's coming down the hill toward us full-force, and then with a turn of the road, it's passing us only a few yards away. It's gorgeous and adds life and spirit to the entire scene. When we reach the top of the canyon, the road straightens, the mountains part, and the lake comes instantly into clear focus.

The water is to die for, smooth as glass. The sun beats down on its surface full-force, with not a cloud in sight. Light reflects in an even blanket from one side to the other. About a quarter of the lake is still hidden as it wraps around the backside of the mountains' edge. That cozy little secret corner is exactly where we're headed. There's a boat dock that will provide a perfect parking place, and then it's a short hike to our intended destination.

Carlos guides the truck into a far east parking slot in the back corner of the lot. We all pile out, in a bit of a hurry to win our bets. There will be no fooling around with this wager. Besides that, everyone aside from Carlos is already starting to catch a buzz. He and Todd muscle their way down the path much faster than Maria and me; we're left behind to breathe in their dust. We struggle through the thick tamaracks that have sprung up every couple of feet. There's quite the obstacle course between us and the water. Did the men just show a lack of chivalry? Perhaps. Is the bet worth it? Well, in their eyes it absolutely is! Which is totally okay with me.

Call us new fashion, but my own personal marriage is partly held together by the glue of healthy competition, and my independent little heart is one hundred percent enticed by that. When it comes to Maria, her determined spirit mirrors mine exactly. Together, our attitudes are a force to be reckoned with. Which is one of the many reasons we're so close.

"Can you believe they just ditched us like that? What dicks," Maria jokes, while she stomps her way through the tall, skin-scratching water weeds.

She has a box of beer tightly tucked under her right arm and is carrying her fishing pole and tackle box in the other. I push my way through, very closely behind her, lugging the exact same items of my own. Sophie trots at Maria's heals, as she's never more than a few feet away, the vicious little guard anyway.

"I know, right?" I agree with her completely. "The least they could've done is pack the drinks. Guess they'll just have to be thirsty all day."

That's a lie and we both know it. Of course I'll share, but it doesn't stop me from the threat. Especially since they're far enough away that they can't hear it. The water is especially low today. Which kind of sucks because it's caused a few dead fish to abandon the water at the bank side. The smell is horrendous! It lingers and swirls through the air and sticks to the miniature hair follicles inside my nostrils. There is no escaping this smell, and it will probably linger in my nose for some time. *Great, just freaking great.*

Our speeding feet carry us far past those pesky dead culprits of the God-awful smell. There's no comparison to the odor of dead fish, especially the really big kind that have been rotting in the heat of the summer sun for days. I even gagged, and so did Maria. By the time we catch up to the boys, they've attached spinners on their lines and are slowly reeling in what must be the latest of at least a dozen casts. Still no fish though, so I'm not at all worried. I'll beat 'em without even trying. I can practically feel the luck crawling along my skin today.

Maria makes her way a few feet away from the rest and

tosses out her line. I slip off my shoes and wade into the shallowest part of the water. After only a few casts in, and not a single bite, the sound of Maria's celebration rings through the air like a chirpy foghorn.

"Ha. Ha. Take that, bitches!" she shouts down the shore toward the rest of us.

I turn slowly in the water, as not to slip. The thousands of tiny pebbles under my toes are extremely slick and the mud sinks with each step, threatening to swallow my feet whole. I couldn't move fast enough to get to her even if I wanted to, so I don't even attempt it. Besides, it doesn't really matter how big it is, I'm sure to out-do her eventually, anyway.

"Hold it up!" I shout in her direction.

I squint my eyes tight, trying to see as she holds her prize high into the air. Not bad, but not really that great either. It's hard to tell from this far away, but I'm sure it's one that'll need to be tossed back, I think with a hint of sarcasm. I can see Todd is walking toward her to help get the hook out.

I turn my attention back to the task at hand, but before I can even cast my line into the water, I hear a tussle. It's an awkward mix of Maria's and Todd's irrational mumbling and cursing, mixed together with excruciating Sophie yips. *Oh crap, oh crap, oh crap, oh crap.* I can tell from the sound that Sophie is hooked, but they're too far away to see just how bad it really is. I move through the water, back toward the shore, as fast as my sunken feet will allow. I slip twice but catch myself before I'm all the way down.

By the time I reach the shore and am able to actually make a run for it, Carlos, Todd, and Maria are together and huddled into a tight little circle around Sophie. I push my way into the circle and the sight of it sucks the breath from my lungs. A giant three-prong fish-hook is lodged securely with one prong in Sophie's paw. And, even more securely, with another prong in

Maria's finger! They are hooked together in the most literal way.

Panic and anxiety ricochets between us, like a bouncy ball at super speed. Anyone that knows anything about dogs is very well aware that Jack Russells aren't exactly the type of animal that you want to be physically attached to, especially while they're afraid and in pain.

Carlos has pulled out a pair of wire-cutters, but Maria's hand is shaking involuntarily, and Sophie is biting the crap out of herself, Maria, and of course any of us who take a shot at cutting the hook to detach the two.

"Somebody just cut the damn hook!" Maria's pissed, rightfully so.

"Give me those!" I order and grab the cutters from Todd.

My attempt at it is even worse than either of the men's had been. The harder we fight Sophie, trying to hold her still and poking at the wounded area, the worse she struggles. The harder Sophie struggles, the deeper this hook sinks itself into both of them.

"Damn it!" Maria cusses again.

She snatches the cutters with her free hand, grits her teeth, and with one swift movement, clamps them shut on the hook. I'm quite sure Sophie's yelps could be heard miles away. The deed is done; they're separated. I reach for Sophie to give Maria a moment to get herself situated, only to be growled and snapped at. I pull my hand away just in time to avoid a serious bite. Sophie is hurt, and there'll be no one allowed to touch her aside from Maria.

"We have to get to a vet and fast," Maria says as she scoops up her dog.

We take a quick, close examination of Maria's finger as well as the dog's paw. The hook prongs are embedded deep into each.

"I think we should try and get this piece of hook out of your finger first or get you to a doctor," I argue. "We can get Sophie to a vet and her paw looked at after, right?"

"No," she protests. "We have to take care of Sophie first. And besides, she isn't gonna let me put her down long enough for my own finger to be looked at. Let's just get the hell out of here."

And so it was, the very beginning of an adventurous day, sabotaged by hook and dog. The would-have-been fishing adventure soon turned into hours of driving, stressing, drinking, hook removing, and heavily sedating a Jack Russell—and was topped off by a bet unfinished. In the end, Maria and Sophie turned out just fine.

STORY THREE
TRAMPLING BEAST, SUPER SHORT PRELUDE TO A PHOBIA

Based on a true story, this super short tale of a phobia offers the humorous insight of a young girl encountering a disastrous event while trying her hand at farm life. The Time Wasters Series brings about several Super Short Prelude Stories (names have been altered to protect identities). In Trampling Beast: While spending time on her cousin's farm, Diedra finds herself making an effort to help guide an escaping animal back to its rightful place. What started out as a slight fear quickly forms into a lifelong phobia of this particular farm animal.

I don't live on a farm. Small town, yes, but a farm, no. My aunt and uncle however, do live on a farm. It's about a fifteen-minute drive from my house to their house. I'm twelve years old now, and their daughter Kelly is thirteen. It doesn't matter that she is only five months older than me, because she insists that it makes her my elder, no matter what, and therefore the boss of everything. The subject is visited often, and I usually just laugh it off and give her a pass; she is my best friend, after all. That said, however, there is the rare occasion when this very subject is cause for war.

Neither Kelly or I have a sister of our own, so being cousins, and together regularly, we've practically adopted each other as such. She is the closest thing I've ever had to a real sister, and I'm the same for her. I have two older brothers and she has one. This makes us both the babies of our families, and we're absolute brats to play the part. The great thing about our closeness is that we are able to beat the living tar out of each other, and then bandage up and embrace in a hug afterward. Which also happens regularly.

It's not an uncommon event to either wrestle each other into submission, or even take hold of kitchen utensils and/or remote controls to use as our choice weapons in an assault. Arm-pinching wars, dirt-heavy fights, and dead-leg competitions are very routine. This might make us sound un-lady like, or even a teeny bit like motherless brutes, but hey, if the shoe fits wear it, right!? Our mothers are actually pretty fantastic to give us space to live so free. Sometimes, we get to act like wild animals, and it's great.

Last night, I slept over at Kelly's farm. Now, the sun's rays are peeking through a crack in the drapes of her bedroom window. The inch wide, straight line of blinding light, lands right on my face. It forces my eyes to squint open and my face to bunch. I groan and roll to my side, hoping to hide from its irritating brightness and heat. Rather than finding comfort, I find the floor, with a very hard *thud*.

"Argh," I groan again, this time a little louder.

Kelly's bed is only a twin size, and rather than sleeping on the hard floor, or couch in the other room, which I sometimes do, I chose to squeeze in the bed next to Kelly. Apparently, our bunched-up snuggle to enjoy the comfort of the mattress didn't quite pay off in the long run. Kelly shoots up into a seated position in one swift motion. You'd think the house was on fire by the panic in her widened eyes and the frantic cranking back and forth of her neck.

"Wha—what happened?" she asks in a frenzy.

I don't need to answer; I just raise my hand. She leans over the edge of the bed to catch me rubbing my head and glaring at the window. An involuntary laugh flows easily from her mouth and she buries her face in a pillow to muffle the sound.

"Shut up Kelly, we're gonna wake up your dad and then we'll both be in trouble."

"It's not gonna be my laugh that wakes him up," she struggles to whisper through her rolling, pitchy giggle. "I'm pretty sure you're falling off the bed shook the whole house."

Kelly's laughter continues to grow, with a failed attempt to keep it in check. After a snort and a cackle, she finishes explaining what's so dang funny. "I was even dreaming about an earthquake." More rolling laughter. "That almost scared the pee out me."

The laughter is contagious and I rip the top blanket from the bed to bury my own face. The only thing worse than waking up to a painful crash on the floor is an annoying case of the giggles. Kelly's dad, my Uncle Ben, works the graveyard shift as a mechanic at a local coal terminal. He's probably only been asleep for an hour or two, so if we wake him up, we'll never hear the end of it.

We'll be in trouble all day long. Meaning no treats, no riding along into town, no friends over and, most importantly, no more sleepovers for at least another week. Waking up Uncle Ben is a definite no-no, which also sucks because he is one of the funniest guys I know. If he weren't sleeping all day during the week, then our free time could be as fun as it is on the weekends, and trust me that's epic.

We successfully muffle our growing laughter until an unavoidable sound of passing gas ruptures out into the air. *Whoops*, I think, but I can't actually say whoops due to the unexpected fart, and my laughter takes a change of pace. It's grown beyond the point of needing a muffle, and has become that awkward silent laugh. My body rolls and shakes but no sound escapes me. Then a high-pitched squeal sounds as I suck in air.

No sooner does my airy squeak break into the air, when the sound of a creaking floor intrudes upon the peaceful silence of the house. All of a sudden, my fluff isn't so funny. Neither is my falling off the bed, or Kelly's dream. I lay frozen, not daring to move, because I just know that somehow even a slight twitch of an arm or cough could ruin the entire day. *Pretend to be asleep, pretend to be asleep,* I chant silently in my mind. Even though I'm on the floor in a clearly uncomfortable position.

The quiet sound of creaking floorboards underneath slow-moving feet pass Kelly's room and continue into the kitchen. *Whew*, that was close. We both let out relieved sighs and giggles, but only small giggles, and then proceed to get our lazy bones up and dressed.

Kelly's brother Derek was the culprit of the wandering feet. We find him sitting at the kitchen table, scarfing a heaping bowl of cereal. It's important to eat breakfast fast on the farm. There is way too much to get done, and even more fun to have outside before the heat of the day sets in. If we don't do chores early, then we're screwed trying to feed and tend water in the blistering sun. Either way, there are jobs to be finished, sun or no sun, so it's best to just get moving as quickly as possible.

Soon enough, breakfast is devoured, and we're running through the chores as fast as possible so that we can play and do whatever we want. It's quickest if we split up. I take the chickens and the dogs, tossing and scooping food at record speed. Kelly waters the horses and cows, while Derek tends to the fields. We'll wait until the evening to take slop to the hogs; they're a good ten-minute walk away, so we decide to wait until later when we can ask permission to take a four-wheeler.

Watering the big animals takes much longer than my choice in chores, so I join Kelly. She's sitting on the top of the fence, straddling the large wood panel at the top. A long green-and-yellow water hose is shoved deep down into one of several large plastic barrels.

"So, what do you say, Diedra? Are you gonna suck it up and ride Buddy today?"

By Buddy, she's referring to a cow. I hate cows. They smell and, for some weird reason, I'm exceptionally intimidated by them. I get a little anxious when I'm too close to one, and I think they can sense it, because they always get skittish when I'm around. I've never come close to a cow that doesn't get jumpy and noisy when I walk too close, so I try and stay as far away as I possibly can. Buddy is the calf that Kelly and Derek chose this year to be their pet. Last year, it was Buddy Sr. and I think it's a safe bet that next year they will have a Buddy Jr.

This year's Buddy was born a little early, like pre-spring, so he isn't exactly a baby anymore, but he isn't a full-grown cow either. He's like a teen in cow terms, which very conveniently makes him the perfect "riding size" according to my rambunctious cousins. I prefer to stay on the safe side of the fence and watch from a healthy distance.

"I think I'll pass," I answer her question with the same reluctancy that I do practically every day. "You guys are retarded."

Kelly chuckles and jumps from the fence. Then, she moves the water hose into the next barrel, a few yards down the fence line. It's the last barrel to be filled and the last of the chores to be completed this morning. As if on cue, I can see Derek coming at us full speed from the far end of the field. He's whooping and hollering and single-handedly chasing the small herd of cows toward us. Mostly, he's pushing Buddy, trying to get him to the fence so that he and Kelly can take turns jumping on his back. It's almost comical watching them hang onto the stupid cow for dear life while he trots around the field trying to shake them loose.

Kelly cranks the water valve shut. It clearly takes everything she has. All eighty-five pounds of her is clenched and flexed. She's bent down at the knees, squatting nearly to the ground, and her elbows are high in the air as she uses their angle as leverage to make up for her lack of muscle mass. I stand back and watch, containing the urge to laugh and poke fun. The debate between helping her and mocking her is playing ping-pong in my head. Ultimately, it's a no brainer, and I opt for letting her struggle, because it is funny. But I do decide to be somewhat nice today and I refrain from the tease. Eventually the deed is done, the water hose is turned off, and she is wiping the sweat from her forehead.

Derek moves to my side and gives me a strong-armed nudge to the rib cage.

"It's funny every time, huh?" he asks and nods toward her.

"Yeah." I let go of the laugh I was trying so hard to hold back. "I thought about helping her this time."

One bushy eyebrow raises questionably on Derek's tanned,

round face. "Well, at least is was a thought, right, Diedra?" he teases.

I nod, with a satisfied smirk.

"You wanna ride Buddy?" he asks.

There is nothing but genuine excitement in Derek's voice, as usual. There's a dirt smudge running across his cheek, but I don't say anything, I just let him wear it. It doesn't matter how many times I tell Derek "no" about riding Buddy, he still asks. Although he's a lot sweeter about it than Kelly is. He doesn't push or tease; he just asks nicely with a kind little twinkle in his dark brown eyes. Maybe he hopes that I'll grow a pair overnight and change my mind, but of course I won't. Ever. Kelly walks up.

"Whatcha' talkin' bout'?" She grins.

"Ridin' Buddy," I answer with a smile and a small roll of my slightly frightened eyes.

"She ain't gonna do it," Kelly barks at Derek, as if he did something wrong.

He responds with a chuckle and playful shove, nearly knocking her off her feet. Nearly ... but she catches her footing and bounces back to the full-of-attitude stance that she had before. Her hands are quickly placed back on her bony hips where they were prior to the push.

"Yeah, yeah," he says. "If we're gonna do this, we better hurry cause I'm gonna have to go in and wake Dad up."

"Why?" I jump in, already knowing the answer.

"There's a hole in the fence, and I couldn't see Big Bertha anywhere. I think she's out."

Crap, oh crap, oh crap, oh crap, I knew it!! The panic of the situation affects me much differently than it does Derek and Kelly. They're able to brush it off, very nonchalantly, and then race to the fence to help each other jump on Buddy. My feet are glued in place. I suddenly feel like I'm going to be sick. I hardly even notice Derek shove Kelly mid-run, sending her tumbling and rolling across the dirt.

I remain in my safe zone while my cousins take turns riding Buddy. Usually, I flinch and cringe and look away, just knowing that one of them would end up with some sort of broken body part. But today is different. I'm distracted, and I hardly even watch. My eyes are glued in space. The lump in my throat slides into my chest, then breaks into tiny pebbles, lodging themselves throughout my ribs and guts in all different places.

Big Bertha is like a whole different breed of her own. She's the bringer of evil, the mother of all shit storms. Big Bertha is the largest, ugliest cow on the face of this planet. She's one of those weird breeds that come out a woman when they should have been a man. She has horns and everything, but no wiener. She's never even had babies because she's too big for any of the bulls to climb on top of. That, and she's got the temper of Satan himself, so any time a bull comes close wanting some lovin', she flips her evil switch and releases the wrath of hell on them. Big Bertha is always alone; it seems like the other cows in the fairly small herd are afraid of her, and rightfully so.

I swear that Big Bertha can sense it when I'm here because she has literally never gotten out when I'm not around. So far this summer, she has escaped three times. The first, I lucked out and my uncle was able to herd her toward Derek rather than me, so I came out of it all in one piece. The second time, I faked sick and was able to stay in the house, pretending to puke. And now here we are—escape number three. I can't very well get away with playing sick again or I'll get caught. I'm going to have to buck up and do my part. The only thing there is for me today is prayer and luck. It feels like my heart is going to escape clean out of my chest.

This is the very reason that I'll never ever be a farmer. I

honestly can't wait until their freezer runs dry and they have to take another cow to the slaughter because Big Bertha is sure to go. She doesn't produce babies, so she is no good. That's literally the only good thing about raising these nasty evil heifers; they make for a pretty dang good steak.

Once Uncle Ben has been summoned from bed, he rubs the sleep from his weary eyes and downs a couple quick mugs of coffee. He jumps onto the four wheeler and makes a couple circles around the property line until he spots Bertha. There is a deep sandy wash that runs along the outer edge of the farm along one whole side. She's in it, strutting around like she owns the place.

We take some time to devise a plan. There are only five of us: me, Kelly, Derek, and my Aunt Emma and Uncle Ben, so it's not going to be easy. We're really going to have to give her hell. If we can't round up this mean old cow, then we'll have to make phone calls and summon help from the Almighty himself. Big Bertha is impossible, and most likely the hardest cow in the county.

The plot goes something like this: Uncle Ben will drive the four wheeler up the wash and push her down a ways until they are parallel to the biggest gate of the corral and ready to push her out. Kelly and Derek will run along the upper outer edges of the wash, waving sticks and yelling so that she won't want to get out. If she does escape the wash too soon, then she will surely take off in the wrong direction and all hope of getting her safely back in the field will be lost.

My Aunt Emma will wait at the turning point where we need to push her out of the wash and I will be standing by the corral, ready to help guide her in. Derek rounds up the biggest stick he can find and shoves it in my arms. It's twice as tall as I am and heavy. I'm not a whole lot bigger than Kelly; what we lack in size we make up for in attitude. I hate to admit it, but my attitude alone is not going to save me today. My legs are shaking and my breath is shallow. I'll be lucky if I don't pass out before Bertha even gets to my checkpoint.

"Here, you're gonna need this," Derek says as he hands me the stick. "We'll all be together by the time she gets to you, so you really don't have anything to worry about. Just wave this stick around so you look big and yell as loud as you can. You'll be fine."

The anticipation is killing me, so much so that I'm starting to pace. My feet are growing tingly and my vision is faltering. It's weird what fear can do to your body's senses; every part of me feels out of whack. After what seems like a lifetime, I can hear it. A multitude of "heahs" and "move its" and "whoops" is moving toward me like a wave of redneck sounds pulsing through the air.

Then, it quiets, and that's when I see her. Big Bertha in all her glory, except rather than run toward the fence next to me, like I was anticipating and hoping for, she stops. *No one else is here! Where are they? Why aren't they guiding her?*

I can hear the four wheeler as it keeps on going down the wash. I can also hear shouting and arguing between Kelly and my Aunt Emma.

I make out one of their shouts. "You lost her?"

"I couldn't keep up, at the side of the wash, she was moving too fast. She must have got out," Kelly shouts back at her mother, defiant and anxious.

Here I am, face to face with Big Bertha. I can hear her breath and see her snot. We lock eyes and she lowers her head in my direction. *Oh my God! She's literally staring me down.* I know I should yell for help. I should let my family know that I found Bertha and, if they run now, we can get her in the gate … but I don't, I can't. My throat is glued shut and my voice has escaped me. All I can do is stand in one spot and shake. Fear and shock courses through my veins, growing more intense with each pump.

Bertha drags her front hooves across the ground, one at a time. I've seen this before in the movies, and I know exactly what is going to happen. *Why the crap does she have to have horns!?* Everything about the burning in her eyes and the forward slant of her head shouts charge. All I can think is RUN! I do just that.

An uncontrollable scream escapes my lungs and I drop the stick and sprint for my life. Sure enough, Bertha charges at me. I make it to the fence with only an inch left between us. She closes the gap in a matter of seconds and slams the fence full-force as I jump. I fall to the ground and back up like a crab—all arms and legs in an awkward scramble to get as far away from this crazed beast as I possibly can!

It's easy to see how she has been able to break out. This animal is utterly unstoppable. Thrashing around the fence like she's possessed. Just as I'm about to either pee or pass out, the rest of the crew come running to my rescue. They'd heard my screams and knew instantly that Bertha was the culprit.

In the end, they were able to get her through the gate and help me safely to the other side of it without getting too close to Bertha so as to piss her off again. She had it out for me, and there was no stopping it. What started out as a small fear of cows has now developed into something bigger. The best possible way for me to explain today's events is to say that it started with a fart and ended with a phobia!

THE END

Dear reader,

We hope you enjoyed reading *Time Wasters #1*. Please take a moment to leave a review, even if it's a short one. Your opinion is important to us.

Discover more books by Didi Oviatt at
https://www.nextchapter.pub/authors/didi-oviatt

Want to know when one of our books is free or discounted? Join the newsletter at
http://eepurl.com/bqqB3H

Best regards,
Didi Oviatt and the Next Chapter Team

WHERE TO FIND DIDI

https://didioviatt.wordpress.com
http://www.goodreads.com/author/show/7207389.Didi_Oviatt
https://www.facebook.com/didioviatt
https://twitter.com/Didi_Oviatt
https://www.instagram.com/didioviatt/
http://amazon.com/author/didioviatt
https://www.bookbub.com/authors/didi-oviatt

Listen to Didi Oviatt's books on Audible:
https://www.audible.com/author/Didi-Oviatt/B00HVJJTLE

Summary of Didi's Books:
Search for Maylee: http://mybook.to/SearchMaylee
Since Maylee was abducted from her high school the very month of graduation, her aunt Autumn has never lost hope in finding her.

It's been three years. Autumn has finally reached inside herself and found the courage to track down an old lead. She travels across the country to find more clues about Maylee's disappearance.

But will she be able to pry Maylee's case back open, and what will she uncover in the process of searching for Maylee?

It's a cold, dark world we live in, and Autumn is about to find out just how cruel it can be. But strength and determination are on her side, and she will do whatever it takes to deliver justice.

Aggravated Momentum: http://mybook.to/Aggravated
After sisters Markie and Kam get tangled with the wrong people at the wrong time, long-buried family secrets begin to emerge.

A serial killer is targeting people close to them. As danger inches closer and closer to home, twisted desires become a reality. The deeper they dig, the darker the secrets they find. But who is the cold, calculated murderer, and can they find a way to survive?

Praise:

★★★★★ - "There is an authenticity to Ms. Oviatt's writing that is refreshing to experience in a thriller-type novel."

★★★★★ - "A murder mystery with plenty of drama, suspense and danger. Fans of mystery and thriller genres will love this book."

★★★★★ - "Fast-paced and full of twists I never saw coming. I was hooked immediately."

Justice for Belle: http://mybook.to/justiceforbelle
Ahnia has a very dicey past - one that is scratching under the surface, just dying to get out.
She's hit rock bottom, broke and desperate to be on top again.
When she finds herself partnering up with man she hardly knows, and who's utterly untouchable, she's forced out of her comfort zone in every way.
Will Ahnia and Mac's dangerous decision be a success, or will she find herself in the clutches of an unforgiving force, brought about by her childhood sin?
In this nail-biting thrill ride, no one is as they seem...and no one is truly safe with those they trust.

Sketch: http://mybook.to/sketch

When local girl Misty is found dead in an underground bunker, the town is thrown into a whirlwind of panic and speculation. Times are tough, but the spaced-out farmer community pulls together as one, trying to uncover who's guilty.

Thrown smack in the middle of the chaos is a group of teens: local troublemakers, but with good hearts. Although they're innocent, the local law enforcers believe otherwise, and the true killer is lurking far too close for comfort.

Will the four be able to uncover the truth before one of them pays the price for Misty's death?

The Suspenseful Collection (Vol. 1):: For Mature Readers Only:
A suspenseful novel with a twist. Eight short stories, by two suspense authors, from diverse backgrounds. From opposite sides of the Atlantic these stories have been created. One author started the tale and the other ended it. No discussion, no pre-planning, but yet their stories are seamless. With just creativity and the use of writing prompts, to craft one tale, with two different writers. This anthology of suspenseful, fast paced and engaging tales covers multiple genres. From heart felt romance, crime, fantasy, and steamy historical fiction. There is a story for everyone!

Steamy Historical Crime Fiction: It was The First Time I Killed A Man.
It's 1972 and New York's first female serial killer Lisa Vanacilli is in the hot seat again, ten years after her conviction of murder to the first degree and innocent plea. The ruthless but sexy reporter Tiffany Low cracks Lisa for a confession... at a price. Lisa is strong, courageous and says it how it is. This story has been extended due to reader's demand. And is only for adult readers.

Psychological Fiction: Every Time I Hear That Voice From The Basement.
George appears to be harmless. The local neighbourhood geek on the outside, married to Jolene. In reality, he's a very disturbed man. His path crosses with Dana, the local check out girl. This is a psychological suspense story with a twist.

Crime Fiction: The Entrance To The Tunnel Is His Only Way Out.
Juan is a wanted man, and an ex-gang member on the run from Atlanta to Mexico. With a hundred grand in cash stolen from his ex-boss, he meets an unlikely fate in Mexico. A fast-paced crime fiction story.

Contemporary Romance: When His Hands Run Up My Thighs I...

Love has no time limit, age limit or use by date. Sarah now in her fifties is reunited with her long-lost love Joshua. They last had contact in 1961. In the present day, thanks to the advancement of technology their paths cross. A heart-warming and modern tale, about long distance love, that will leave you warm inside.

Suspense: We Only Said Goodbye With Words, I Died A Hundred Times:

In 1963 Russian Femme Fatale Mila Petrov is London's top Madam. Her entertainment house is booming, she has a team of London's strongest women behind her. Unfinished business from her past creeps up and haunts her. It's nothing she can't handle. A suspenseful historical tale, with a strong femme fatale.

Fantasy: The Ones Who Live At The Bottom Of The Ocean, Come To The Surface.

A beautiful coming of age story, featuring sixteen year old Zoe and her mother May-Li. Myth becomes reality, as Zoe finds out who and what she really is. Her mixed descent reveals more than what meets the eye. This fantasy story is set against the backdrop of a Greek island and Hong Kong, China.

Suspenseful Crime Fiction: Guilty As Charged, In Self-Defence

California's sassy, tough, and likeable defence lawyer Catherine has taken on a case so high profile, if she wins she'll become a partner of Martin Law Firm. Defending forty six year old Mrs. Chevelle. An ex Las Vegas show girl, now a Hollywood wife, on trial for the murder of her high-profile husband. She claims she's innocent. Readers are taken on a fast-paced journey on a mission to seek the truth.

Contemporary Fiction: It's A Man's Man's World:

A beautiful modern tale showing the love and appreciation of a woman. James Brown said it right when he said, "it's a man's man's world, but it would mean nothing without a woman or a girl."

Blurred Lines (The Suspenseful Collection Vol. 2):: For Mature Readers Only:

As the second installment of suspenseful short stories by two suspense authors, from diverse backgrounds, Blurred Lines offers a thrill ride with nine stories in genres across the board. From opposite sides of the Atlantic these stories have been created. One author started the tale and the other ended it. No discussion, no pre-planning, but yet their stories are seamless. With the use of writing prompts Kim and Didi have created tales that will tug at your heart strings, drop your jaws, and leave you clinging to the edge of your seat. From gory horror, romance, crime fiction, family drama, and fantasy, there is a story for everyone!

Crime Fiction, Psychological: "I'm Back Bitches, Now Panic!"
Lynn McCarmick has spent six years behind bars for a crime she didn't commit, although she's a far cry from an innocent woman. Her once loyal team of con artists set her up for a robbery that landed her a long term home in a Scottish prison. After an early release for good behavior, Lynn is finally able to let the bad bitch inside of her roam free.

Contemporary Romance: Heart of Gold
In this star crossed, light hearted tale, two people with the purest of hearts, each long to find a mate who is giving, honest and real. A heart-felt romance.

Psychological Thriller, Slasher Romance, Erotica: Chainsaw Ridge
Alice is one of a kind, and was raised by a nasty man with killer habits. After an accident rendered the awful man disabled, everything changed. With an ultimate twist, this gory tale takes Alice and her husband on one hell of a bloody adventure. Due to popular demand this story was extended!

Investigative Crime Fiction: Crime Scene Investigation
Detectives Flynn and McBride are on the case of a murder. Owner of the Chinese restaurant where the body was found, Mr. Wang, is devastated. The pressure is on to find the killer and to clear Mr. Wang's establishment as a safe place for his patrons. The detectives piece together outside connections that are weaved into Mr. Wang's ties, in a very delicate way. Is there more to the murder than what meets the eye?

Historical Fiction: A Miracle Baby Story
In a tragic tale of tough love and loss, brought about in a western setting, two young lovers are frowned upon by nearly everyone around. Adsila is a teen of Cherokee descent, who falls for a young cowboy. In a bitter-sweet tale she fights for the survival of herself and unborn child in a community filled with hate and judgement.

Paranormal Suspense: A life Gone?
Franklyn Poppy, is a husband and father who found himself in a place between life and death. He becomes a loathly witness to the woman he loves having an affair with his twin brother.
He's introduced to the infamous dark Goddess, Maman Bridgette who shares his disdain for the happenings with his wife. The outcome for Mrs. Poppy and her fateful intertwining with this powerful Goddess is powerful and resonating.

Metaphysics, Clairvoyant, Thriller: Murder by Mistake

The Wilkinson family consists of an Air Force father, a loving mother, and two daughters Anna and Julie. They are polar opposites, and Julie, the younger of the two has a special gift. She's able to see things before they happen. When she's mentally the witness to a murder that's yet to be solved, she's forced into action in an altercation with the killer.

Fantasy: Witchful Thinking

Gretchen isn't your average witch, as she was born into a clan descending from the blood of Fate herself. Growing up in foster care was an intentional way for her to find her own path in using her magic, as she's intended to be a tool for Fate's use. A twisty tale set in the present and past day.

Family Drama: Real Mom

After the abandonment of their mother, twins Josephine and Jerilynn are taken in by their new stepmom, and become the big sisters to quite the large and quirky family. During a family vacation the two team up, and try to uncover the mystery of their estranged biological mom.

New Age Lamians: http://mybook.to/newagelamians
Jackson has barely reached manhood when lightning heralds the end of the world as we know it. The lightning has awakened the Lamians: descendants of the mythological creature Lamia.
In his world, The Company delivers supplies into his village, and harnesses technology that others lack. Soon, Jackson is taken by The Company; he is to be an ultimate warrior, alongside few others, as their blood is rare and compatible with the technology needed to transform them.
According to The Company, the Lamians are monsters who need to be defeated at all costs. But is Jackson really the one who can save the world?
Praise:

★★★★★ - "A twisty, intoxicating read."
★★★★★ - "Genuinely imaginative."
★★★★★ - "*Compellingly entertaining*"

Time Wasters #1
ISBN: 978-4-86750-512-0

Published by
Next Chapter
1-60-20 Minami-Otsuka
170-0005 Toshima-Ku, Tokyo
+818035793528

6th June 2021

www.ingramcontent.com/pod-product-compliance
Lightning Source LLC
LaVergne TN
LVHW090040080526
838202LV00046B/3890